W9-BKH-683

Traditions of Faith

The Story Behind Our Favorite Christmas Carol

Silent Night, Holy Night

Written by Myrna Strasser
Illustrated by Guy Porfirio

Zonderkidz

Zonder**kidz**.

The children's group of Zondervan

www.zonderkidz.com

Silent Night, Holy Night
ISBN: 0-310-70672-6
Copyright © 2004 by Myrna Strasser
Illustrator copyright © 2004 by Guy Porfirio
Requests for information should be addressed to:
Zonderkidz, Grand Rapids, Michigan 49530

Library of Congress Cataloging-in-Publication Data

Strasser, Myrna.
  Silent night, holy night : the story behind our favorite Christmas
carol / Written by Myrna Strasser ; illustrated by Guy Porfirio.
    p. cm.
  ISBN 0-310-70672-6 (hardcover)
 1. Gruber, Franz Xaver, 1787-1863. Stille Nacht, heilige
Nacht--Juvenile literature. 2. Carols--History and criticism--Juvenile
literature. I. Porfirio, Guy. ill II. Title.
  ML3930.G84S86 2004
  782.28'1723--dc22
                        2004000318

All Scripture quotations, unless otherwise indicated, are taken from the HOLY BIBLE, NEW INTERNATIONAL READER'S VERSION ®.
Copyright © 1995, 1996, 1998 by International Bible Society. Used by permission of Zondervan. All Rights Reserved.

All rights reserved. No part of this publication may be reproduced, stored in a retrieval system, or transmitted in any form or by any means—
electronic, mechanical, photocopy, recording, or any other—except for brief quotations in printed reviews, without the prior permission of the
publisher.

Zonderkidz is a trademark of Zondervan.

Editor: Barbara J. Scott
Art Direction & Design: Jody Langley
Production Artist: Merit Alderink

Printed in China
04 05 06 07/HK/5 4 3 2 1

To my Strasser nieces and nephews:
Bryce, Brent, Karna,
Lori, Julie, Cory,
Jill, Jodi,
Nathan, Timothy, and Micah
I'll never forget your wide-eyed attention and silly giggles
as you listened to Auntie Myrna's tall tales.
Love you always!

Special thanks to my editor Barbara Scott
for coaching me through the writing process.
God directed her as she directed me, and I am supremely blessed.

—M.S.

To my family, friends and the true spirit of Christmas.
—G.P.

"Grandpa, please sit next to the fireplace," Anna said. "Mama and Daddy, you sit there on the sofa." Anna and her brothers and sister had prepared a special Christmas program just for Grandpa Strasser, who was visiting them in Chicago all the way from Germany.

Grandpa settled back in Mama's comfortable rocking chair and sipped hot cocoa. "Ah, just like the old days. The Strasser children back on stage!"

The children looked at each other, wondering what Grandpa could mean, but they didn't ask. They were too eager to start the show.

First, Peter recited the Christmas story from the Gospel of Luke. Then Marta played her piano recital piece. Tommy stood on his hands while his puppy stood on its hind legs, and Anna pirouetted like a ballerina. To end their program with a grand flourish, the four children sang Silent Night in four-part harmony.

Grandpa clapped his hands. "Wonderful! Wonderful! How did you know Silent Night is my favorite Christmas carol?"

"Mama told us," Peter said.

"Did she also tell you the song is known all over the world because of a singing family named Strasser?"

"Hey, that's our name!" Peter said.

"That's right," Grandpa said. "In fact, my great-great-grandfather was the oldest boy of that singing family."

"I know him!" Peter said. "We have his picture upstairs in the hall. He has lots of whiskers."

Tommy counted on his fingers, "That would be my great-great-great-great-great-grandfather, right Grandpa?"

"A lot of whiskers and greats, to be sure," Grandpa said with a chuckle. "But this Strasser family was really special. They even sang for the King of Prussia."

"A king? Really? Wow!" Marta said.

"It's quite a story," Grandpa said.

"Time for a story! Time for a story!" Anna clapped her hands, jumping up and down.

Grandpa sipped his hot chocolate, smacked his lips, and said, "It happened many, many years ago in Oberndorf, a little village near the city of Salzburg in Austria."

"I know where Austria is," Tommy said. "They have lots of downhill ski champions."

"Indeed, they do." Grandpa said.

"Well, a story is told that one winter afternoon," Grandpa continued, "a very sad Pastor Joseph Mohr barely noticed the beautiful Christmas decorations in St. Nicholas Church. All he could think about was the broken organ."

"A broken organ at Christmas." Peter said. "How terrible!"

"They used to say it was mice." Grandpa said, smiling.

"Mice?" The Strasser children said in unison.

"How could mice break the organ?" Tommy asked.

"By chewing holes in the bellows," Grandpa explained. "In the old days, you had to pump air through the pipes with bellows to make the sounds. But that could have been easily fixed. Today many think it was the dampness caused by flooding from the nearby Salzach River. The organ parts simply rusted shut. Pastor Mohr was so disappointed. No music on Christmas Eve."

Marta sighed. She couldn't imagine a Christmas without music. "What did he do?" she asked.

"What could he do?" Grandpa said. "There was no time to get it repaired before Christmas, so Pastor Mohr decided to go home. But one of his church members, John the Woodchopper, met him at the door.

"The woodchopper told him, 'I have happy news, Pastor. My wife just had a baby boy! Will you come to our house and give him a blessing?'"

"Pastor Mohr was such a good man, and said he would be glad to go," Grandpa said. "It was bitter cold, so he put on an extra shirt under his coat to walk through the deep snow into the hills."

"Why didn't they just take a snowmobile?" Tommy asked. Mama nudged him with her toe and then he grinned, "Oh, yeah. I guess they didn't have snowmobiles back then." Everyone laughed.

"Tell us what happened then, Grandpa," Marta said.

"Well, it took a little while, but finally they arrived at the cabin," Grandpa said. "As soon as he stepped inside, he saw Maria rocking the new little baby in the moonlight. He held the baby and prayed that God would protect the little boy. Then he put the baby in the cradle and whispered, 'Sleep in heavenly peace, my child.'"

"How sweet!" Anna said. She snuggled against her mother's shoulder.

"On his way home, Pastor Mohr really didn't notice the cold," Grandpa continued. "It was such a beautiful, peaceful night. Stars spattered the clear sky, and bright moonlight shone down to light his path.

"Crunch! Crunch! His footsteps sounded in the snow. Pastor Mohr talked to God as he walked."

"I do that sometimes," Peter said.

"That's wonderful, Peter. Well, the more he thought," Grandpa said, "the more the beautiful night reminded him of another family. Can you guess who that was?"

Mama smiled at Daddy, but the children wrinkled their brows and thought and thought but couldn't think of anyone.

"Who?" Anna asked.

"It reminded him of the wonderful night so long ago when Jesus was born," Grandpa Strasser said. "Then more words came to his mind. 'Around yon virgin, mother and child, holy infant so tender and mild.'"

"By the time Pastor Mohr reached home, he had written a poem. Even though it was very late at night, he kept writing. He didn't finish until four o'clock in the morning."

Peter yawned. "That makes me tired just to think about it," he said.

"Later that day Pastor Mohr's friend, Franz Gruber, came for a visit. Mr. Gruber was the village schoolteacher and the church organist."

"But the organ was broken," Tommy reminded Grandpa.

"I know," Grandpa said, not giving away the ending of the story. "He asked Mr. Gruber to look at his poem, and the schoolteacher thought it sounded like a song. He asked if he could take it with him.

"When Mr. Gruber left, the pastor thought about what he would say during his Christmas Eve sermon. He would tell how God sent his son Jesus to be born in a manger, and he prayed, 'Thank you, Lord, for this good news I can tell the people.' Even if they didn't have music, they would still have Jesus."

"After the opening prayer on Christmas Eve," Grandpa said, "Pastor Mohr heard the sound of music. He looked up and saw Franz Gruber coming down the aisle of the church, strumming his guitar. Several children followed him, singing Silent Night. The congregation clapped their hands with joy. They would have special Christmas music, after all!"

"Oh, I'm so glad," Marta said. "But what's that got to do with the singing Strasser family?"

Grandpa set his empty mug on the table. "Well, after Christmas, a repairman came to fix the organ. When he finished, he asked Franz Gruber to play something. Herr Gruber played Silent Night, and the organ builder and repairman, Karl Mauracher, thought it was so beautiful that he memorized it."

"Just like I memorized for my piano recital," Marta said.

"Exactly. When Herr Mauracher, got back to his home in Ziller Valley, he played the song at his church. In the audience that day were two singing families—the Rainiers and the Strassers. They both began to sing the song when they traveled. Our Strasser family had four children who sang everywhere...at the schoolhouse, in the city square, even in concert halls."

"Were they kids just like us?" Peter asked.

Grandpa stroked his mustache as he thought, "Well, I suspect they were. Except there were three girls and one boy."

"Did they sing Silent Night?" Anna asked.

"Oh, yes, all over the country." Grandpa said.

"Wow!" Tommy said. "Were they like rock stars?"

"Not exactly," Grandpa laughed. "They mainly sang at merchant fairs."

"What's a merchant fair?" asked Peter.

"Since they didn't have shopping malls in those days, the merchants sold their products at fairs," Grandpa explained. "Sort of like the giant flea markets you have in Chicago. They set up booths to sell all kinds of things...from hats and shoes to plows and wagons."

"What did the Strassers sell?" asked Tommy.

"Goatskin gloves," Grandpa said. "Each time the family went to a different city, the Strasser children would stand by their father's booth and sing."

"Why?" asked Anna.

"People would stop and listen, and then they would buy some gloves." Grandpa said. "Whenever the children sang Silent Night, the people shouted, 'More! More!'"

Mama poured more cocoa into Grandpa's mug as he continued. "Wherever the family traveled that year, they sang their song. One evening at the end of the summer, the Strasser family received a surprise invitation."

"I like surprises," said Tommy.

"What was it?" Marta asked.

"It was from the king," Grandpa said. "King Frederick William the Fourth of Prussia invited the Strasser children to sing for him."

"I'd be so nervous," Peter said.

"They were, but they did it anyway." Grandpa said. "The whole family dressed up in their very best clothes and went to the palace.

"What would you say if you were asked to sing for the President at the White House?" Mama asked the children.

"I know what I'd say." Marta stood up and fluffed her long brown hair. "Mama, does my hair look all right?"

Mama laughed and joined the playacting fun. "And I would say, 'You're beautiful, dear. And Tommy, come here and let me straighten your tie, and don't fidget so much. Goodness, how did you get that smudge on your face?'" Their mother pretended to rub a dirty spot off Tommy's nose. He giggled.

Grandpa chuckled, "That's probably exactly how the Strassers acted. But the children sang as sweetly as they could, thinking about the baby Jesus."

"Did the king like the song?" asked Peter.

"Oh, indeed! He loved the song so much that he declared from that day forward that Silent Night would be sung every Christmas at the Royal Palace.

"And when the Strasser children grew up, they taught the song to their children, and their grandchildren taught it to their children, and the song traveled all around the world. Just think, as Strassers, you're part of a very special history."

Grandpa leaned forward in his chair, "But most important, this song is also special because it tells us so clearly what Christmas is all about. Do you know what message is given every time someone sings Silent Night?"

"I know!" Peter said excitedly. "Christ the Savior is born. That means one silent night, God sent his Son, Jesus, to be born in a manger. The shepherds came running, the Wise Men followed the star, and the angels sang."

"I'm so glad Jesus came," Anna said.

"And I'm so glad you know Jesus as your Savior," Grandpa said.

"Let's sing it again!" Marta said.

So as the fireplace glowed, the Christmas tree lights twinkled, and the puppy's tail wagged, the whole family sang their favorite Christmas carol...Silent Night.

Ideas for Caroling
Silent Night

~ A few days before your caroling party, plan a
baking night. Make homemade cookies and arrange them on
paper plates. Wrap the plates in cellophane and tie them up with
pretty Christmas bows.

~ Before you set off for caroling, tie bells on your coat sleeves
and around your ankles. As you walk along, you will jingle with the joy of
Christmas. Or dress up in costumes. Bright red scarves will also add a festive
touch to your caroling.

~ Appoint a leader who can start the singing at each place you go. Plan the
order in which you will sing your Christmas carols, and make sure your group knows the
words.

~ At each caroling stop, sing your songs and present a plate of fresh-baked cookies.
Don't forget to say Merry Christmas when you finish!

~ Carry flashlights as you walk from place to place or carry battery-powered candles.
Hold them high while you sing.

~ If your streets are free from ice and snow, tow a wagon stacked up with your cookie
plates, or if you have enough snow, pull sleds as you go caroling. On one of the sleds,
fasten a small Christmas tree. Decorate the tree with battery-powered lights and gather
around the Christmas tree while you sing.

~ Make arrangements with nursing homes or a hospital for your group to come
and carol. Some shopping malls welcome carolers. Check with the management to
get on their schedule. Take advantage of the opportunity to pass out invitations to
your church Christmas activities.

After an evening of caroling, gather back at the church or someone's
home for refreshments. Serve hot cocoa, hot cider, and spiced
tea. Chips and dips are always a favorite and easy to serve.
Or for a more complete meal, serve hot chili or soup
with crackers and cheese or homemade bread
and end the evening with apple pie.
Yum!